THE PRINCE
and the
Li Hing Mui

Sandi Takayama

Illustrated by Esther Szegedy

3565 Harding Ave. • Honolulu, Hawai'i 96816 • (808) 734-7159 Fax (808) 732-3627 • www.besspress.com

Once upon a time, on an island in the middle of the ocean, there lived a princess who loved the taste of li hing mui more than anything else in the world. She sprinkled li hing powder on everything she ate. And in between meals she nibbled on li hing seeds. No one could ever remember her real name, and so she was known far and wide as Princess Li Hing Mui.

When Princess Li Hing Mui was old enough to be wed, the king and queen were determined that she marry none other than a real prince. But they had no idea how to go about finding one. One evening, while searching through all the Books of Wisdom, the queen suddenly yelled, "Aha! According to a Mr. H. C. Andersen, we must pile twenty featherbeds on twenty mattresses, and at the very bottom of the pile we must place a pea and . . . "

Just then Princess Li Hing Mui, who had been listening at the door, burst in and cried, "A pea? But I hate peas! I despise peas! Please, oh, kind-hearted mother, anything but a pea."

"Very well," sighed the queen. "No peas. Instead we'll place a . . . "

"A li hing mui?" suggested the princess hopefully.

"Yes, yes, a li hing seed," continued the queen. "A li hing mui at the bottom of all the featherbeds and mattresses. A true prince will feel the seed and be unable to sleep a wink all night."

Every night from then on an eligible young man from one of the best families in the kingdom was invited to the castle for dinner and a sleepover. Each one slept peacefully atop the featherbeds and mattresses.

Princess Li Hing Mui was secretly relieved that none of the young men had passed the test. Many of them were quite arrogant, almost obnoxious. True, they did not complain about the royal bed, but they complained about everything else, from the temperature of the bathwater to (gasp!) the taste of li hing mui. As the months passed, the king and queen despaired of ever finding a true prince for their daughter.

Then one day there was a terrible storm. The normally sunny skies darkened. The rain poured down and the wind howled about every-where. In the middle of the storm, someone knocked at the castle gate. The guards opened it and outside stood a young man. Water dripped down his weatherbeaten hat and ragged clothes. He was clearly a commoner from the village. Still no one could be turned away during such weather. He was admitted inside.

The young man proved to be delightfully entertaining. He conversed intelligently on a wide variety of topics and made everyone laugh with stories of life in the village. He also loved the taste of li hing mui and swore his popo made the best li hing mui on the island. By the time night came, the princess thought she might be falling in love with the young man and pleaded with her parents to let him sleep on the royal bed and see if he could pass the test to be a prince.

"What will it hurt?" said the king and queen, who secretly liked him much better than any of the other young men who had stayed overnight.

At breakfast the next morning, Princess Li Hing Mui eagerly asked the young man, "How did you sleep? How was the bed?" Much to her disappointment, the young man answered, "Oh, I wen' sleep real good. T'anks, eh, fo' da bed!" And indeed he did look well rested. Princess Li Hing Mui consoled herself with the thought that he could not leave until the stormy weather subsided and perhaps still might pass the test. But every morning he looked refreshed and answered politely that he had slept very well.

On the last morning, Princess Li Hing Mui crept quietly into the young man's room. She was now definitely in love with him and wished to gaze upon his face once more before he left. Upon entering the bedroom, she discovered that he was not in his bed at all but upon a single featherbed on the floor!

"What is the meaning of this?" exclaimed the princess.

The young man awoke at her question, blushed, and hung his head down.

"Well?" asked Princess Li Hing Mui anxiously.

"Sorry, eh, princess, I nevah like make trouble," stammered the young man.

"I no could sleep on da royal bed, so I wen' go sleep on da floor."

"Why weren't you able to sleep on the royal bed?" questioned the princess, with a glimmer of hope in her heart.

"Nah, I no like say notting. You guys, you stay so nice to me. I no like make like one grouch."

"Your honest answer would mean a great deal to me," said the princess.

Knowing he could not refuse Princess Li Hing Mui's request, the young man sighed and said, "Get one . . . one lump in da bed."

And seeing the smile on Princess Li Hing Mui's face, he gathered courage and continued, "Only one small-kine lump, but, sheesh, no could sleep. I guess 'cause I just one common guy I stay more used to da floor. Sorry fo' make so much humbug. I go get my stuff and go already."

Princess Li Hing Mui gave a great yell and jumped into the young man's arms. The king and queen and everyone else came running into the young man's room to see what all the noise was about. When they heard the story, they all agreed that the young man was a true prince. Not only did he feel the li hing mui under all the featherbeds and mattresses—he never ever complained of it.

And so Princess Li Hing Mui and the young man were married. And since no one could remember his real name, he became known far and wide as Prince Li Hing Mui.

And as for the li hing mui, it was placed in a koa frame and put on display in the best li hing mui shop on the island. (Prince Li Hing Mui's popo opened her shop after the royal marriage.) The li hing mui is still there today. If you don't believe me, go and see it for yourself.

Glossary

li hing mui   preserved plum, a variety of crack seed, or Chinese candy, much loved by children in Hawai'i. Princess Li Hing Mui would have a variety of sweet-salty li hing–flavored goodies to choose from today, in addition to the mui, or seed: powder, Gummi candy, cakes, syrup, shave ice, popcorn, and arare (Japanese rice cracker).

popo   Chinese term for "grandmother."

Look for other Hawai'i fairy tales
by Sandi Takayama

"Run, run, fast as you can! You no can catch me, I'm one musubi man!" Like the gingerbread man in the classic tale, the musubi man is determined not to be eaten. He leads his pursuers on a merry chase, until he reaches the ocean and has to match wits with a surfer. The surprise ending, like the rest of the story, has a uniquely Hawai'i flavor.

Mango Boy dreams of becoming a sumotori and knows he could be a champion if he had the chance. But while his brothers go off to sumo practice, he has to pick, peel, and slice mangoes. Will he ever get a chance to prove himself? Be prepared for hilarious surprises as you read this delightful Cinderella story complete with Hawai'i-style versions of the fairy godmother, glass slipper, and happily-ever-after ending.

3565 Harding Ave. • Honolulu, Hawai'i 96816 • (808) 734-7159 Fax (808) 732-3627 • www.besspress.com